Aurora Books, an imprint of Eco-Justice Press, L.L.C.

Aurora Books
P.O. Box 5409 Eugene, OR 97405
www.ecojusticepress.com

LIttLE BIG Bear
By Andre Royal Sr.
Illustrated by Andre Royal Jr.

Library of Congress Control Number: 2020938I64
ISBN: 978-I-945432-39-2

LIttLE BIG Bear

A Clumsy Bear fell fast asleep...
While playing a game of hide and seek

By Andre Royal Sr.
Illustrated by Andre Royal Jr.

A Clumsy Bear fell fast asleep
while playing a game of hide and seek.

He'd slept through all ….and much of next fall.
When he awoke and searched for his friends…. He
found he'd lost them all.

Many moons had passed since he saw them last.
He'd better move his paws and move them fast.
Nos-ily he peeked around the bend…
"Where can they be?" he said curiously.

"How long of a nap was took?
How will I and my friends now look?
When I am looking over there…. are they
looking over here for me?
Maybe I should sit still atop this hill
so I can see?
Will it be High enough for me to be seen
from across this ravine?"

"Who knows?" Little Big Bear supposed.
"Will they recognize me?"

"If I am facing forward, will they approach from behind me?
If I stay and continue to play in the shade,
Will they come and find me?"

"THAT'S IT!...THAT'S IT!
COME OUT…. COME OUT!
WHEREVER YOU ARE!"

"How about another game of hide and seek?
We can play right here
Right alongside this creek!"

"GRRRRRRR!" He growled. "How long should I wait?
In the meantime in between time I'm getting sleepy.
HOW LONG SHOULD THIS TAKE?
Maybe I'll take a nap …. OR just a little break?

"The day is running out of sun and it's probably
time to go.
Maybe I should claw a note on this leaf,
Or leave a message about my plans to be up here
in this tree?"

Climb on up! I'll be right here waiting.
Signed…..

Sincerely,
ME.

Andre Royal Sr.

Artist at heart who's entire life has revolved around food. Born on Thanksgiving, His fondest memories were made in the Kitchen - which included drawing pictures for the fridge door. When he's not writing recipes, he's writing stories, or otherwise on another taste adventure.

Photo by Sarah Andrews

Andre Royal Jr.

Andre Royal Jr. Freelance artist born in California - now residing in Oregon. Loves making custom hand crafted longboards, designing logos, creating conceptual designs and working with various styles of artistic expression. Any medium he's challenged with, he makes the most of.

Photo by Andre Royal Sr.

CPSIA information can be obtained
at www.ICGtesting.com
Printed in the USA
BVHW010946120820
585937BV00012B/22

9 781945 432392